Librarian's
Night Before Christmas

Librarian's
Night Before Christmas

By David Davis
Illustrated by Jim Harris

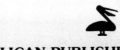

PELICAN PUBLISHING COMPANY
GRETNA 2008

*For all the overworked underpaid librarians. Also, for the Four Star Critique
Group and Nina Kooij, my editor. Finally, in remembrance of James Rice,
Debra Deur, and Chris Halsrud. They left us too soon.—D. D.*

First printing, February 2007
Second printing, March 2008

The word "Pelican" and the depiction of a pelican are trademarks
of Pelican Publishing Company, Inc., and are registered in the
U.S. Patent and Trademark Office.

Library of Congress Cataloging-in-Publication Data

Davis, David (David R.), 1948-
    Librarian's night before Christmas / by David Davis ; illustrated by Jim Harris.
        p. cm.
    ISBN-13: 978-1-58980-336-7 (hardcover : alk. paper)
    1. Librarians—Juvenile poetry. 2. Libraries—Juvenile poetry. 3. Christmas—Juvenile
poetry. 4. Santa Claus—Juvenile poetry. 5. Children's poetry, American. I. Harris, Jim,
1955- ill. II. Title.
    PS3554.A93344L53 2006
    811'.54—dc22

                                                            2006001444

Printed in Singapore
Published by Pelican Publishing Company, Inc.
1000 Burmaster Street, Gretna, Louisiana 70053

LIBRARIAN'S NIGHT BEFORE CHRISTMAS

'Twas a cold Yuletide evening, and I wandered the stacks,
Shelving multiple titles that the patrons brought back.
We toiled overtime at our library here,
'Cause the powers that be cut our staffing this year.

They spent pork-barrel money like a tidal-wave sea,
But no funds trickled down far enough to reach me.
Our books numbered few and were falling apart,
And I sat mending pages with a crestfallen heart.

Still, I answered the phone with Christmas good cheer,
And supplied all the names of the North Pole reindeer.
I slumped addled and weary in my Yuletide apparel;
I felt like Bob Cratchit in *A Christmas Carol*.

Like old Robert Frost, I gazed at the snow,
And longed to be home by the fireside's glow.
I pondered the debate on *Huckleberry Finn*.
Had the love of great books come to an end?

What happened next didn't seem to be real,
'Cause out of the sky cruised a red bookmobile!
Up to the front steps flew this library ride,
With a portrait of Shakespeare airbrushed on the side

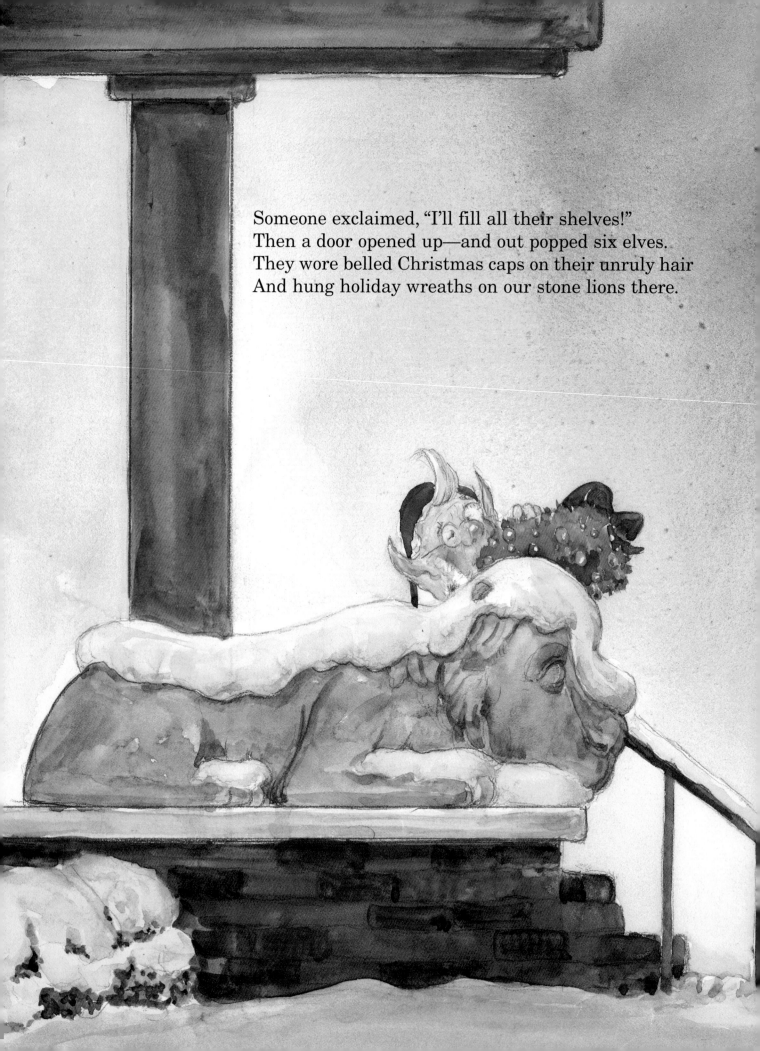

Someone exclaimed, "I'll fill all their shelves!"
Then a door opened up—and out popped six elves.
They wore belled Christmas caps on their unruly hair
And hung holiday wreaths on our stone lions there.

Santa charged through the door, and his black knee
  boots shone.
He bowed as he asked, "Need interlibrary loans?"
Flummoxed and flustered, I fumbled about.
I didn't know whether to check books in or out!

This oldster wore crimson; his fedora was green.
He was bodyweight challenged (if you know what I mean).
He was bearded and gabbed like a good storyteller,
And he grinned like a writer with a New York bestseller.

Nick was jolly and droll; a white mane crowned his head,
And I could tell by his diction he was very well read.
"This place needs some cheer, so let's make a start."
Then he whistled in elves pushing loaded book carts.

They stocked Hawthorne, Jane Austen, Steinbeck, and Millay,
And for the more macho, they supplied Hemingway.
They shelved new science fiction and tomes from the past
And sneaked in romances for sweet Molly McNast.

Nick signed Newbery winners and starred Caldecotts.
Each child got a book, which delighted the tots.
He read stories to children by our small Christmas tree,
While one little tyke took a snooze on his knee.

Elves poured steaming hot chocolate in bright
   Christmas mugs
And rolled out soft carpets to replace our frayed rugs.
They fixed leaks in the ceiling and patched the
   cracked wall
And hung a large portrait of Mark Twain in the hall.

Nick chided a censor, who wished some books gone,
And suggested she scan *Fahrenheit 451*.
For the book-budget cutters, Old Claus had no plan,
'Cause *if* they could read, they just read Ayn Rand.

The elves catered a feast straight from the North Pole.
They carved turkey with trimmings and buttered hot rolls.
Nick nibbled a drumstick, gave his tummy a pat,
And tossed a small portion to the library cat.

They organized goodies so we couldn't miss them
(According to Dewey and his decimal system).
I thanked the old elf for the wonderful show.
He nodded and whispered, "It's time that I go."

After checking his watch, he paid overdue fees,
While folks promised to read—and unplug their TVs.
With these library gifts, my world shined much brighter,
But this crew had a schedule, "a bookman all-nighter."

Nick winked at the cat as they dashed down the aisles
And yelled, "Happy reading, you bibliophiles!"
He loaded his crew and sang from the yard,
"The best gift of all is a library card!"

His ride lifted up and flew over the gate.
And just to show off, he zoomed a fast figure eight.
Nick boomed from his book van, "Do one more good deed.
Have a *real* merry Christmas—teach someone to read!"

Merry Christmas!